For Kate D.B.

Ta Louis, with love, Rosi x

EGMONT

We bring stories to life

First published in Great Britain 2009
by Egmont UK Limited
239 Kensington High Street
London W8 6SA

Text copyright © David Bedford 2009
Illustrations copyright © Rosalind Beardshaw 2009

David Bedford and Rosalind Beardshaw have asserted their moral rights.

ISBN 978 14052 3032 2 (Hardback)
ISBN 978 14052 3033 9 (Paperback)

1 3 5 7 9 10 8 6 4 2

A CIP catalogue record for this title is available from the British Library

Printed and bound in Singapore
Colour Reproduction by Dot Gradations Ltd, UK

In Love

David Bedford * Rosalind Beardshaw

EGMONT

One bright day, Morris the mole
peeped out of his hole
to find that it was Spring.

"Yippee!" said Morris.

Then he hopped
down from his hill
and went off to find
someone to love.

Morris peered
around the farmyard.

Moles don't see very well.
But Morris didn't think it would
be hard to find someone to love,
because he knew just what to look for . . .

Shiny black fur.

Luscious shiny black fur!

Morris hugged the
Luscious Shiny Black Fur.
He was
in love!
Morris blew
his love a kiss.

But when the
Luscious Shiny Black Fur
blew him a kiss back . . .

Morris was blown off his feet!

He landed in
a pile of leaves – but
nobody came to see
if he was all right.
"Ouch," Morris said
to himself, feeling glum.

Then Morris
smelled the
first new flowers
of Spring.

"Yippee!" he said and skipped
out of the leaves and went off to
find someone else to love.

A
pink
nose.

A pretty pink nose!

Morris hugged the
Pretty Pink Nose.
He was
♡ in love! ♡
Morris rubbed noses.

But when the
Pretty Pink Nose
rubbed back . . .

Morris was sent rolling awa

old
and wet
and slimy
from
head to toes!

He landed in some mud - but
nobody came to see if he was all right.
"Ouch," Morris said to himself, feeling glum.

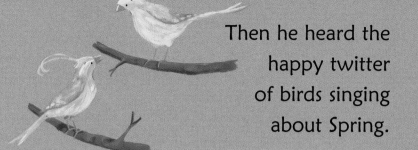

Then he heard the
happy twitter
of birds singing
about Spring.

"Yippee!" said Morris, and he jumped
out of the mud and went to find
someone else to love.

Big
wide
feet.

Gorgeous
big wide
feet!

Morris hugged the
Gorgeous Big Wide Feet.
He was
in love!
Morris sat down in the
meadow with his love.

But when the
Gorgeous Big Wide Feet
sat down too . . .

Morris wa

choked and tickled by feathers!

"Atishoo!" he sneezed, tumbling backwards.

This time he landed on a sharp thistle – but nobody came to see if he was all right.

"Ouch," Morris said to himself, feeling glummer than ever.

"Ouch, ouch, ouch!"

And even though he knew it was still Spring,
he went back and sat on his mole hill.

Morris said to himself,

"It is Spring and I am alone without love.
Shiny Black Fur was too rough.
Pretty Pink Nose was too wet.
And **Gorgeous Big Wide Feet** made me sneeze.
I looked for love and I didn't find it."

Suddenly Morris heard a tiny voice.
It said,
'You have not looked hard enough!'

And before he could blink . . .

. . . someone gave
him a **present**.

The present balanced
on his nose

and wrapped
around his ears.

And when Morris
looked **through**
his present, he saw
very clearly . . .

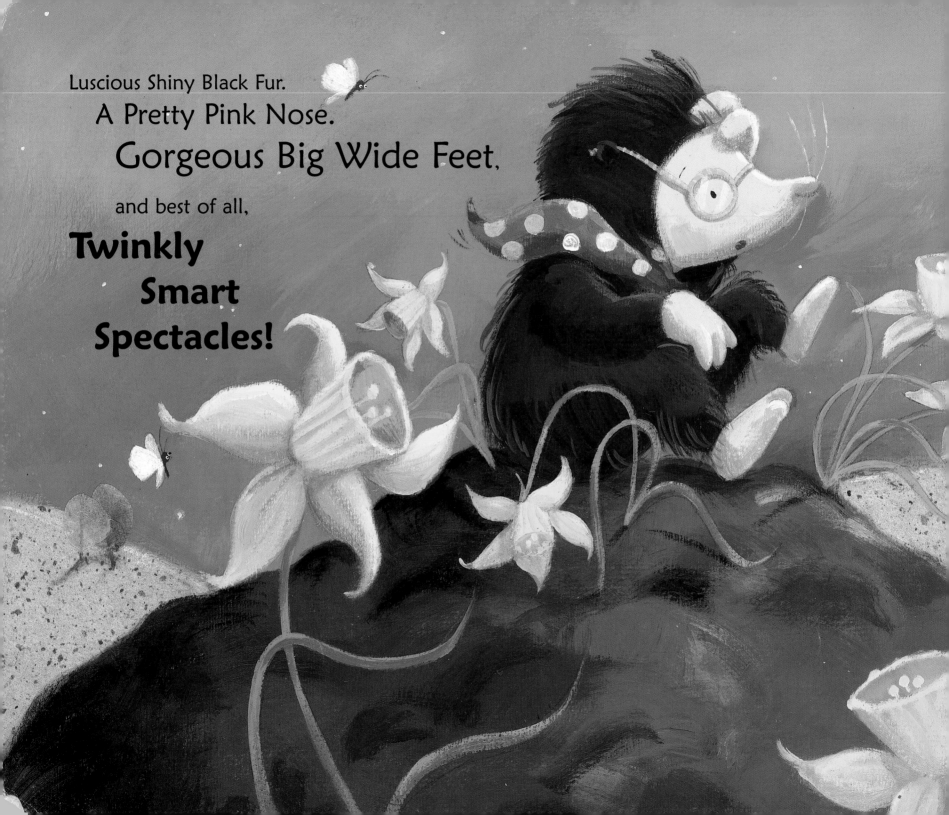

Luscious Shiny Black Fur.
A Pretty Pink Nose.
Gorgeous Big Wide Feet,

and best of all,

Twinkly
Smart
Spectacles!

"I'm called Mini," said the tiny voice,
as Morris stared at her.
"Are you all right?" she asked.

And Morris said,

"Yes I am!"

Morris hopped down
from his hill.
But he wasn't looking
for love any more.

Love had already found him.